Go Smiley, go Smiley, go, go, go! Search your way through this crowd of lively motor fans to locate the missing Smileys. The race is nearly over, so try beating the clock by finding these 8 Smileys before the last tickety-tock!

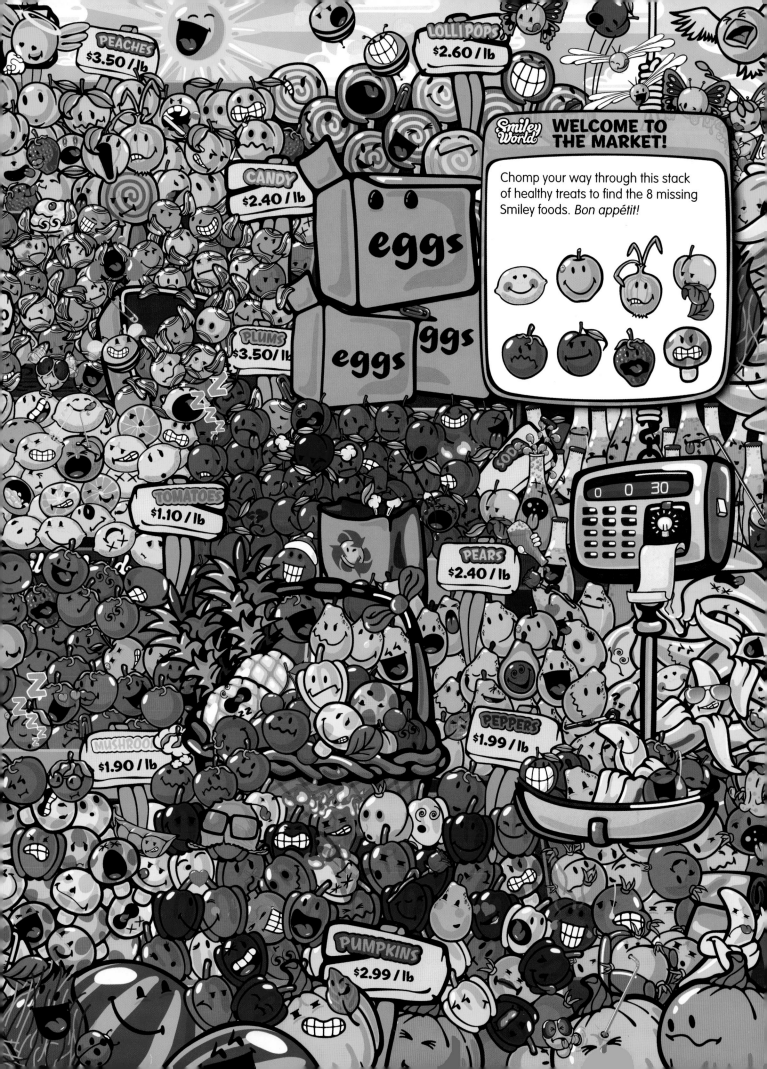

What an amazing party! All the Smileys are dancing at the concert of the century! It's happening at every level. Why not join in? But don't forget to find the 8 special partygoers for the most fun!

Menu
Cool-bean beats
Scary scales
Deep sea bass

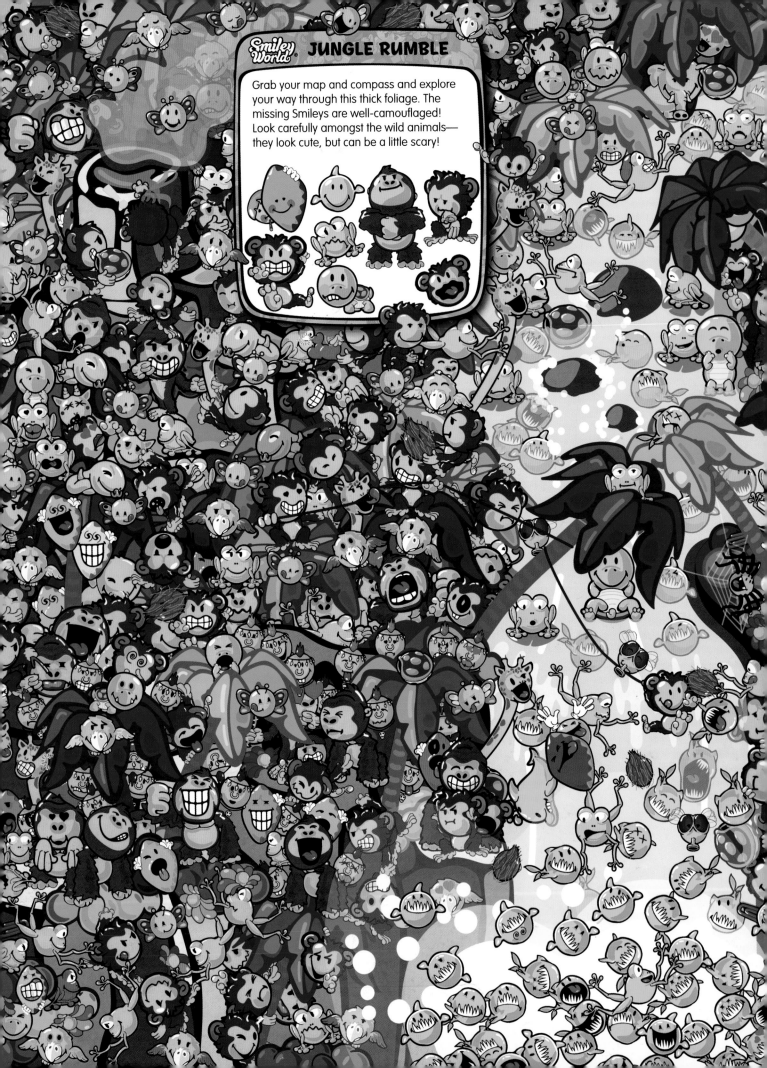

JUNGLE RUMBLE

Grab your map and compass and explore your way through this thick foliage. The missing Smileys are well-camouflaged! Look carefully amongst the wild animals— they look cute, but can be a little scary!

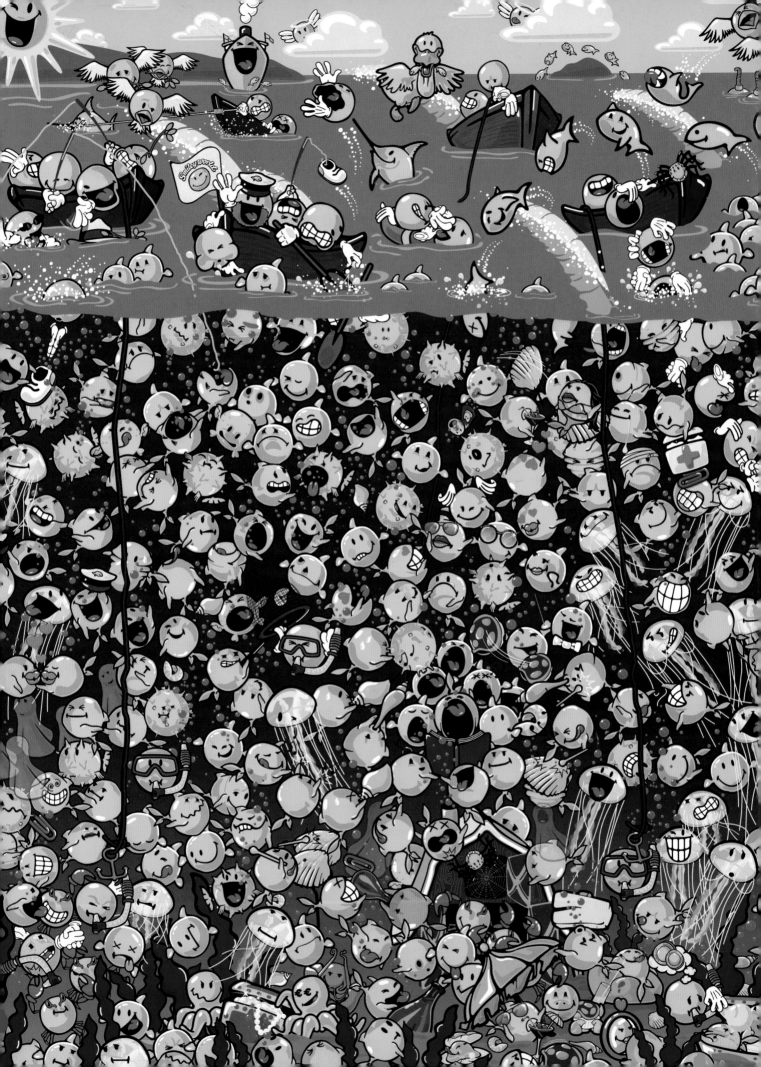

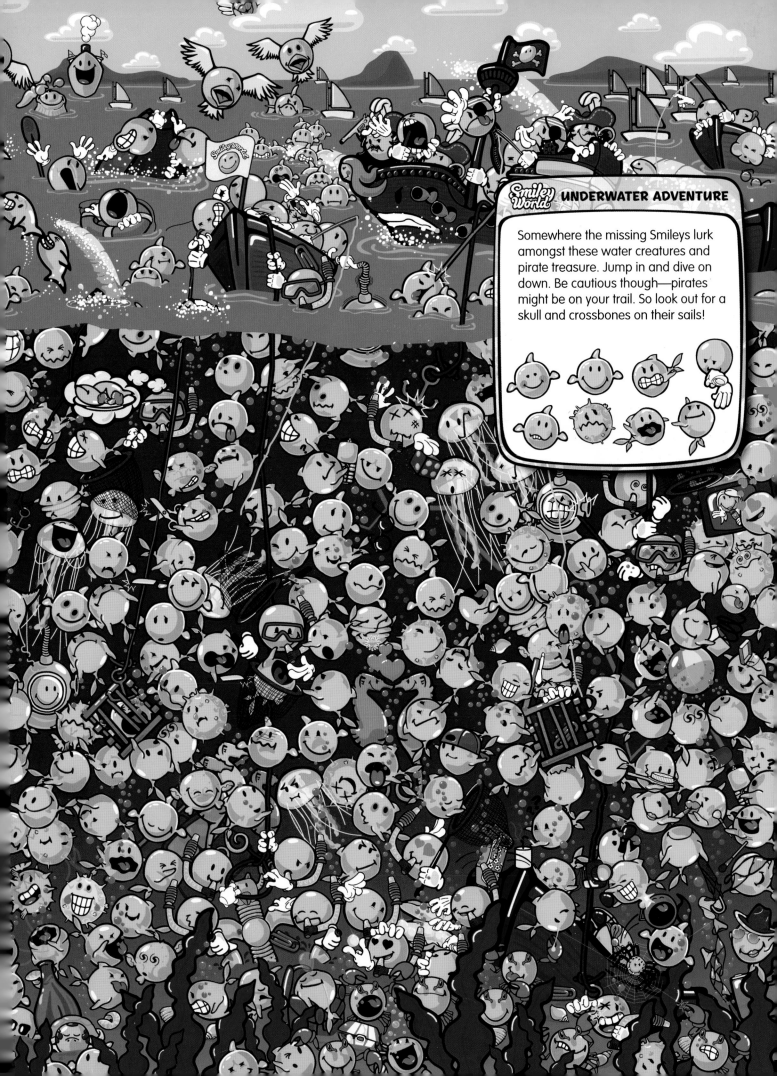

UNDERWATER ADVENTURE

Somewhere the missing Smileys lurk amongst these water creatures and pirate treasure. Jump in and dive on down. Be cautious though—pirates might be on your trail. So look out for a skull and crossbones on their sails!

Smiley World — CHITCHAT TIME

Choose your screen name and chatter your way through each fun-packed room and conversation—it seems everyone is doing it these days! Find the 8 missing Smileys amongst this babbling network of cyber chin-waggers!

ATTIC

CALL CENTER

POOL HALL

LOUNGE

10 TON

WORK SITE

CORRIDOR

CLASS

GYMNASIUM

ENTRANCE

CONCIERGE

THE HAPPY FLORISTS

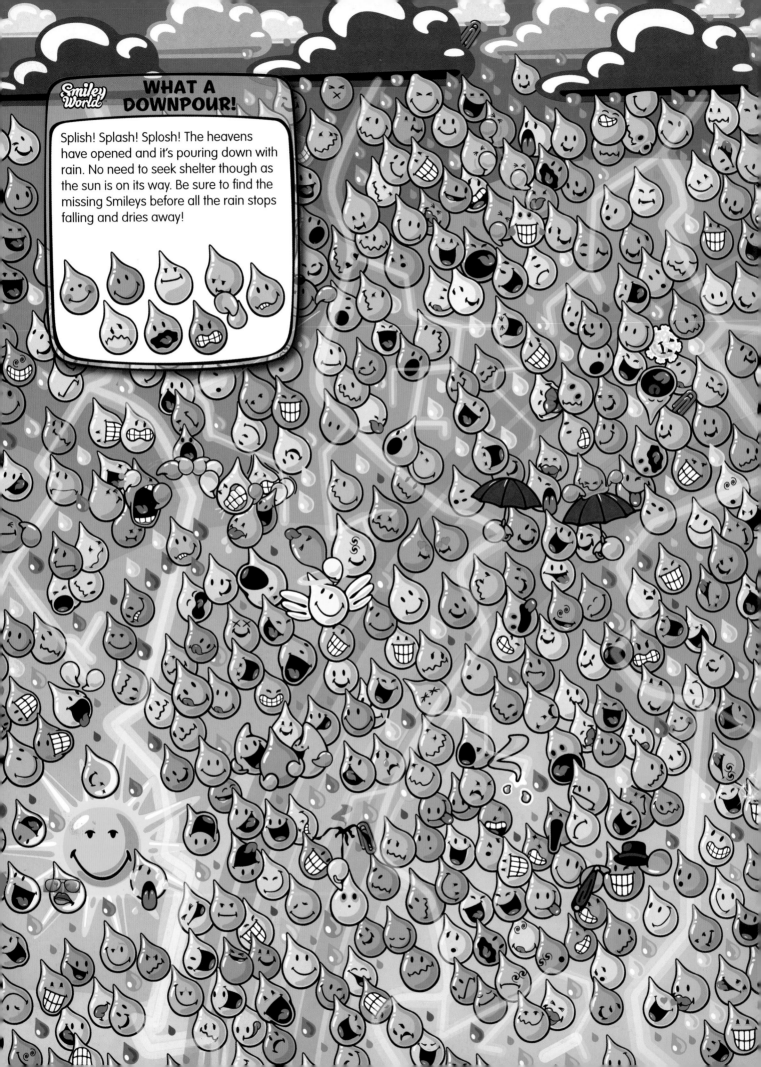

WHAT A DOWNPOUR!

Splish! Splash! Splosh! The heavens have opened and it's pouring down with rain. No need to seek shelter though as the sun is on its way. Be sure to find the missing Smileys before all the rain stops falling and dries away!

THE HEROES OF SPORTS

Smileys are meeting at the Grand Smiley Stadium for the Worldwide Smiley Games. But the virus has upset them—all the athletes have lost their sense of direction! Can you find the lost Smileys in the middle of all this chaos?

CRAZY FOR POLLEN

It's a horticultural festival frenzy as Smileys everywhere are enjoying the hot sunny weather. There are 8 rare flowers that need to be picked out before the end of the show—can you help?

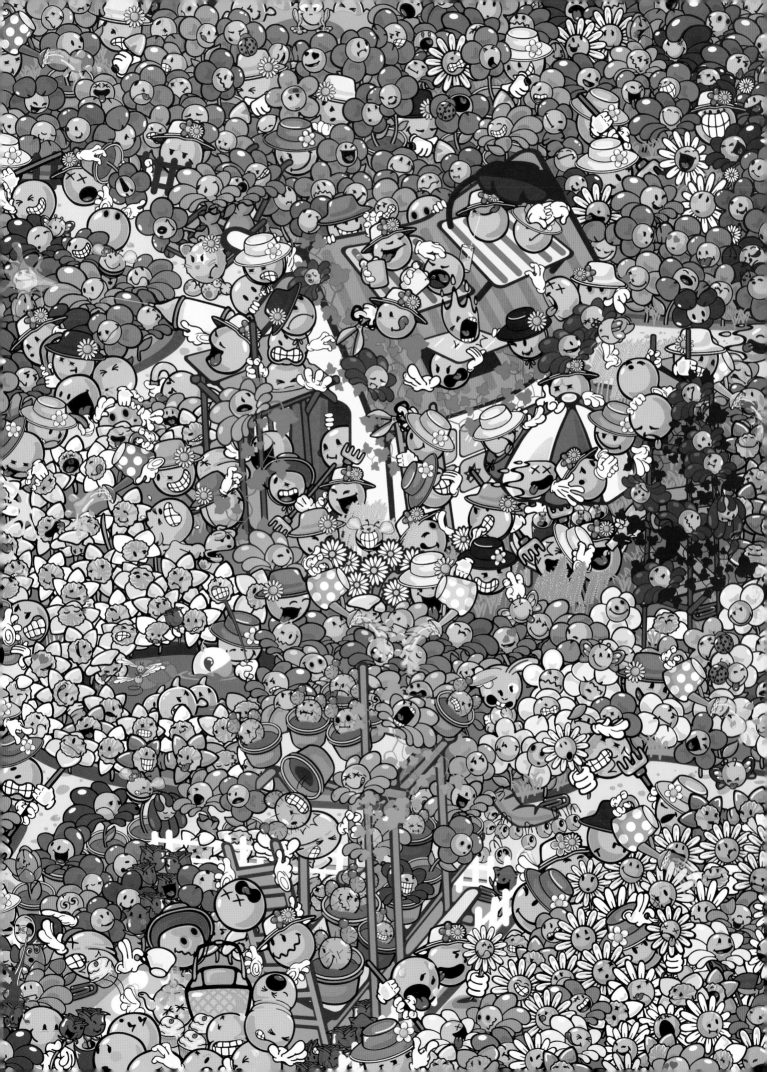

TOO MANY COOKS!

Whoa! Too many cooks are spoiling the broth! All of SmileyWorld's chefs have been dumped into one steamy kitchen. The place is a melting pot of emotion. Find our Smileys before this pickle gets served!

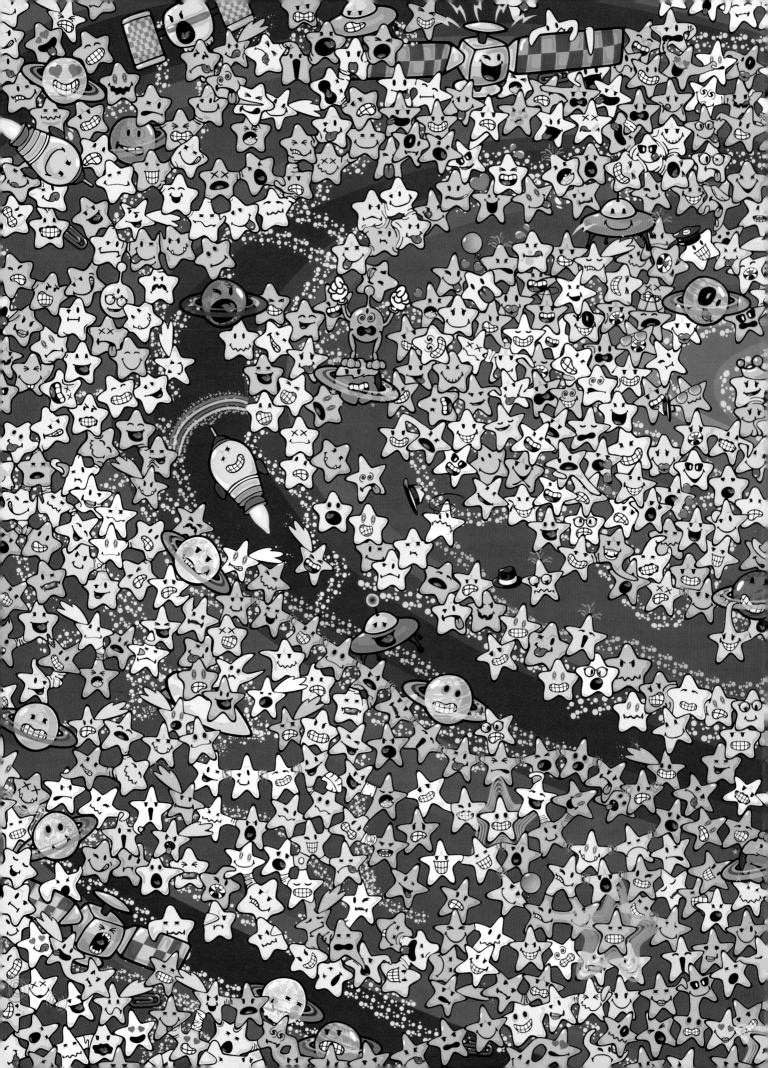

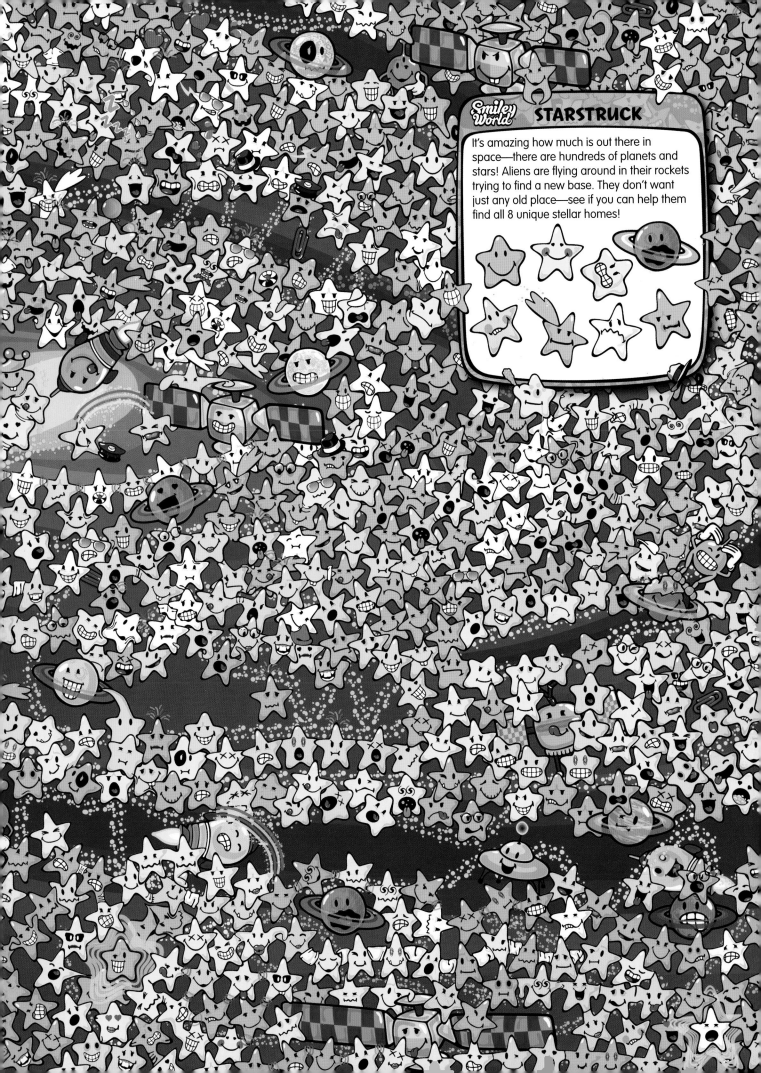

SmileyWorld STARSTRUCK

It's amazing how much is out there in space—there are hundreds of planets and stars! Aliens are flying around in their rockets trying to find a new base. They don't want just any old place—see if you can help them find all 8 unique stellar homes!

Smiley World — SMILEY GALLERY

Emotions (Anger)
anger · resentful · cross · agitation · vexed · evilness · annoyance
bitter · madness · rabid · scorn · irritation · disgust · sourness

Emotions (Fear)
scared · shock · alarm · cower
nightmare · anxiety · hesitant · panic
defensive · insecurity · trapped · intimidated

Personality Traits
dimwitted · suave · babyish · thoughtful
anonymous · dirty · shortsighted · greedy
cheeky · greedy · stinky · hypnotized
loser · angelic · goofy

Symbols
positive · speech bubble · recycle
peace · poison · heart
throw away litter · recyclable · think bubble

Animals
cat · dog · chick · frog · goat · panda
fox · ladybug · fish · raccoon · camel · tiger

Characters
angel · pirate · monster
alien · Al Capone · Albert Einstein

Emotions (Thought)
topsy-turvy · confusion · ambivalence
thought · distrust · denial · indecisiveness
distracted · interest · unconvinced

Occupations
astronomer · priest · scientist
professer · police officer · captain
airline pilot · astronaut · artist
clown · nurse · soldier

Emotions
in love · narcissism
admiration · adoration · ardour
kindness · liberation

Emotions
happy · engrossed · tickled · sleep · excitement

Actions
black-eyed · advise · blow bubblegum · concentrate · congratulate
funny face · halt · whistle · zipped
wake up · obey · high 5 · kiss · play flute

Transport
taxi · bus · car · sailboat · locomotive
submarine · train · balloon · airship · flying saucer · truck

Food
apple · biscuit · strawberry
cheese · mushroom · coconut

Important Info
These Smileys are part of a dictionary of more than 1,700!
www.smileyworld.com

Emotions — Shame

shame | mortification | regret
dejection | embarrassment | disgrace
apologetic | uncomfortable

Sport

football | baseball | golf | darts | volleyball
rugby | basketball | fitness training | skiing | snorkling

Smiley 1
Smiley 2

daisy | daffodil
tree | pansy
Neptune | cactus

Alphabet & Numbers

A B C D E F G
H I J K L M N
1 2 3

Weather

sun | spring | autumn
freezing | clear night | summer

Love

goodness | peace loving | encouragement
friendly | pacifist | acceptance
concern | consideration | sentimentality
loyal | sympathy | thankful

Emotions — Confidence

confidence | cool | courage | pride
resolve | certainty | hope | emphatic
eagerness | smug | expectation | anticipation

Nations

Austrian | French | Australian
Turk | American | Japanese

Flags

France | Japan | Spain
Great Britain | Italy | Mexico
China

Objects

alarm clock | cell phone | bomb
house | television | bag
present | crossword puzzle | vase

Descriptive

flattop hair cut | pea brain | block head | nose piercing
double chin | goatee | got the flu | wearing a black tie
working till 5am | wearing a cycling helmet | wearing a bowler hat | braces

Happiness

welcoming | friendly wink | crazy | playful
exuberance | guiltless | triumphant
highly amused | delight | joy | tears of joy
festive | exhilaration | bliss | delirium
impressed | merriness | hyped | relief

Occasions

birthday | Easter | Halloween
Valentine's Day | Christmas | winter
Father Christmas | graduation | New Year's

Emotions — Sadness

upset | hurt | deceived | miserable | stung | sadness
despondence | sick | fed up | grief
hopelessness | crushed | disillusionment | homesick | depression

Smiley World
BONUS MISSIONS

New Message

File Edit View Insert Format Tools

Get Mail   Reply   Send   Attach   **B** *I* <u>U</u> A

To: You Again!
From: Smiley World
Subject: **SPECIAL MISSION**

Well done, your mission is almost completed! All that is left to do is attach the Smiley icons you have collected to this e-mail and send it back to SmileyWorld.

Instructions:
You may have noticed that amongst the websites you have searched there are special red paperclips. These are for attaching the missing Smileys to your e-mail. There are 8 in every scene, one for every missing Smiley. To do this you will have to find the golden SmileyWorld @ symbol, hidden somewhere in this book!

Good luck with your mission,

Smiley World
Smiley Communication Center
www.smileyworld.com

Concert of the Century

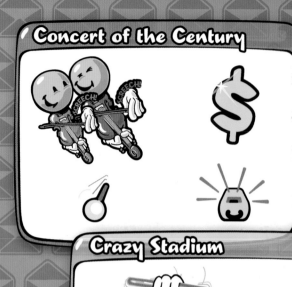

Crazy Stadium

Welcome t

Congratulations!

You have completed **Stage 1** of your assignment. SmileyWorld is very impressed with your seek-and-find skills and therefore has selected you to comlpete and extraspecial mission.

Stage 2 requires you to find and collect the Smileys and props shown here on this screen. But hurry, the virus is tracing your search. Spot the Smileys before they are deleted!

Good luck and happy hunting!

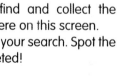

Special Items

@ x 1   paperclip x 96

Information Highway